Story Illustrations
by Geri Stewart

Cover Design & Computer Art
by Dan Poynter

*Happy Reading!
Kay Hoflander*

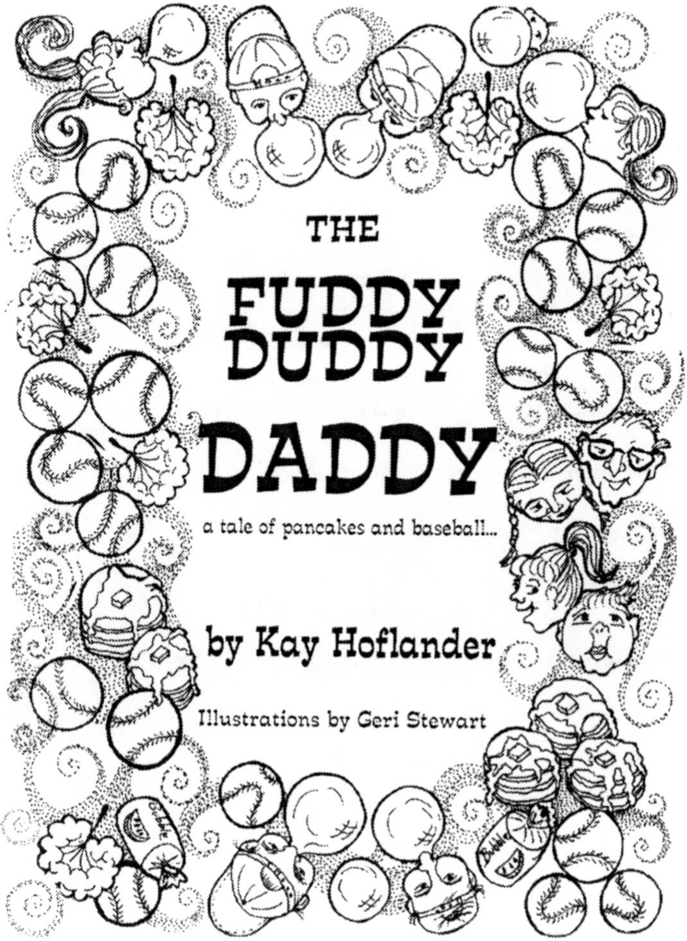

THE

FUDDY DUDDY DADDY

a tale of pancakes and baseball...

by Kay Hoflander

Illustrations by Geri Stewart

authorHOUSE®

AuthorHouse™
1663 Liberty Drive, Suite 200
Bloomington, IN 47403
www.authorhouse.com
Phone: 1-800-839-8640

First published by AuthorHouse 10/5/2007

ISBN: 978-1-4343-3881-5 (sc)

Library of Congress Control Number: 2007907390

Printed in the United States of America
Bloomington, Indiana

This book is printed on acid-free paper.

For all my pancake-lovin' and baseball-playin' kids and grandkids.

Contents

Stars of the Story

In Jackson Point, nearly everyone has a nickname.

Richard Austin Maxwell, 9 years old, nicknamed Pancake because pancakes are his favorite food.

Thomas Arlen Vincent II, 10 years old, nicknamed Hoppy. He is Richard's best friend who has always been called Hoppy, but no one remembers exactly why.

Lita Gail Maxwell, 8 years old, nicknamed Skippy. She is Richard's little sister who Richard says is always disgustingly happy and skips everywhere she goes.

Vanessa and Valerie Vega, 8-year-old twins and best friends of Lita Gail. Skippy nicknamed them Van and Val for short.

Mr. Maxwell, Richard and Lita Gail's Dad, sometimes called Cotton but only by Mrs. Maxwell.

Mrs. Maxwell, Richard and Lita Gail's Mom. Mr. Maxwell is the only one who calls her by her full name, Carolina Mary.

The Stars of the Story

Lita
Gail
Maxwell

Mr. Maxwell

Richard Austin Maxwell

Caroline
Mary
Maxwell

Valerie and Vanessa Vega

Thomas Arlen Vincent II

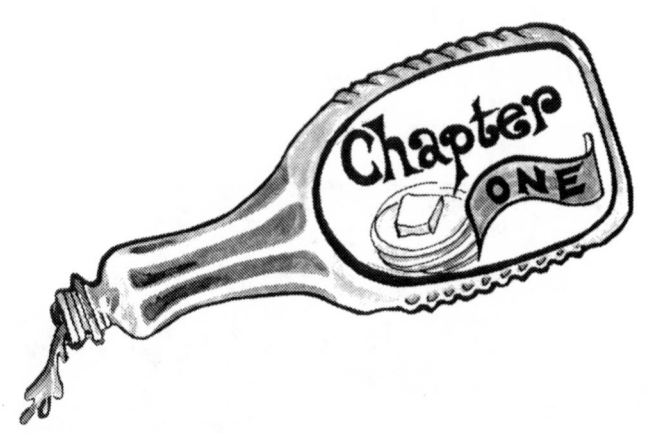

Time to Get Up

Pancake heard his Dad calling from the foot of the stairs, "Richard Austin. Lita Gail. It is time to get up!"

Richard (known to just about everyone in Jackson Point as Pancake) groaned and covered his head with his baseball comforter. He loved it. Grandma and Grandpa gave it to him for Christmas. Somehow it made him feel better today, but he was not exactly sure why he needed to feel better. Pancake just knew that he was sleepy and not ready to get up. As usual, lots of thoughts started to roll around in his head. Richard was always thinking.

"I wish Dad would not call everyone by their full name," Richard thought. "He even calls Mom by hers--Carolina Mary. Everyone else calls her Carol."

Then he remembered what was wrong. It was Mom! Mom was gone. His heart sank. She left that morning on an early flight to visit his grandparents. Grandpa was having an operation, and Mom went to help Grandma.

Pancake felt sick to his stomach. He missed Mom already, and he had not even had his breakfast yet.

About then Richard's sister Skippy came bouncing into his room in her usual good mood that never failed to make Richard mad. Skippy's real name was Lita Gail. Pancake wished Skippy were not so cheerful in the mornings. He wished she would leave him alone. Especially today!

"Skip," he said, "it is gonna be terrible around here without Mom for a whole week, and I do not need you makin' it worse."

It seemed as though nothing ever bothered Skippy. She was not even sad about Mom leaving.

"Are you OK Pancake?" Skippy asked.

"Sure, I am fine, but I wish Mom was here. Dad is so serious all the time. We are going to have a lousy week. It will be awful with Dad in charge," Pancake complained.

"Sounds like you are whining again to me," said Skippy. "Why don't you hurry up and come down to breakfast. Dad's making your favorite—pancakes!" Skippy left the room singing as usual.

That is why Mom nicknamed her Skippy, Pancake thought to himself. Lita Gail was always happy, and she skipped everywhere. At least that is what it seemed like to him.

Richard liked the nicknames Mom gave them. She called him Pancake because that was his favorite food, and no matter how many he ate, he never tired of pancakes.

Richard was thinking about Mom and how she sometimes called Dad by a nickname. She said Dad's friends called him "Cotton" when he was a boy. She said Dad liked it. Pancake did not think he did.

"Richard Austin Maxwell. Get down here now!" said Pancake's dad in a loud I-mean-business voice.

Pancake had his own secret nickname for Dad. As Richard dressed hurriedly for school, he thought about it again. What would Mom and Skippy think if they knew what he really wanted Dad's nickname to be?

Fuddy Duddy Daddy!

Chapter 2

Half a Cup of Milk

Pancake felt a little better after breakfast. That was because Skippy was complaining about her breakfast. As they walked to the corner to catch the school bus, Skippy was mumbling something about not letting Dad help her tomorrow with her breakfast. Most of the time she did not complain, but this morning was different.

"Dad measures the milk for my cereal and will not let me have more than half a cup," groaned Skippy. Then she added, "He says I have to have just the right ratio of milk to cereal. Yuk! It is too dry that way.

At least, Richard, you do not have to go through the cereal ritual. Maybe I should switch to pancakes, too."

Pancake was not impressed with Skippy's problems because he was remembering some of Dad's other odd ways that seemed far worse, such as filling the bathtub a third full of water. Mr. Maxwell would say, "That is enough water for anyone."

"Well, maybe it is," Richard thought, "but it is no fun that way. When Mom is here she does not mind if I fill the tub full. She says she likes it that way, too."

He was remembering even more of Dad's fuddy duddy ways and dreading them when his pal Hoppy arrived at the bus stop. Hoppy's real name was Thomas Arlen Vincent II. Dad told Hoppy once that with a name like that he could be a banker or an attorney because important sounding names help you get ahead in the world.

Hoppy preferred his nickname, even though no one remembered how he got it.

"What's with the long faces?" Hoppy asked.

"Mom has gone to visit my grandparents for a whole week and Dad is in charge," Pancake explained.

Skippy interrupted Pancake before he could say any more. "We love Dad," she said, "but he has some really strange ways of doing things." Skippy felt bad about criticizing Dad, yet even she had to admit, Dad was driving her nuts.

Hoppy did not ask any more questions. Instead, he began talking about P.E. class and baseball starting today. He sounded excited.

Skippy waved to her friends Vanessa and Valerie Vega who were walking very fast in the next block. Van and Val, as Skippy liked to call them, were usually late for the bus. Today was no exception. Skippy ran to meet them.

The twins were identical, and Pancake could not tell them apart. Skippy could though. The three girls were in the same grade at school, but Valerie was in a different classroom. The twins had been in different classes since preschool because the school would not let them be together. Once Skippy had Valerie in her class and that was fun. She wished they could all three be together every year. They could not. The school would not allow it. "Rules, rules, rules," Skippy sighed.

The three girls and the two boys were daily bus stop buddies, but more importantly, they were friends all year round because they all lived near Chautauqua Park. The park was one block wide and one block long, not a big park as parks go, but then neither was their town. Jackson Point, Missouri, had only 1,142 people, or at least that is what the sign said on the road coming into town.

Sometimes Pancake and Hoppy would pretend they did not want to play with Skippy and the twins, but they played anyway. Skippy knew that Pancake and Hoppy really did like to play with them, and she knew that all of them enjoyed playing together more than they did with most of the other kids in town. It had always been that way.

"Why don't you guys come to our house after school," suggested Skippy.

Pancake started speaking before the others could answer, "No, Skippy, that is not a good idea. Remember Dad will be there. He is coming home early from work all this week while Mom is away. We are stuck with Fuddy Duddy Daddy."

"So what's the problem with that?" reacted Hoppy angrily.

Mr. Maxwell told Richard once that Hoppy never had much to say, but when he did it was really important and Richard should listen to him.

Still angry, Hoppy added, "At least, you have a dad!" That was something Hoppy had never said before, not even to his best friends.

No one breathed a word as the bus pulled up to the corner. Richard felt sick to his stomach, again.

Chapter 3

Hot Box Practice

By the time school was over for the day, Richard and Hoppy forgot the conversation about their dads at the bus stop that morning. They decided at recess to meet Skippy and the twins at Chautauqua Park to have "Hot Box" practice after school. Each of them would get a turn at stealing bases. Richard loved the game. He was feeling good when he walked home, dropped off his books and lunch box, and headed straight to Chautauqua Park. Besides, he thought to himself, since Dad was not home yet he would not have to answer "stupid" baby questions about what his day at school was like.

Since Chautauqua Park was one block wide by one block long, it was the perfect size and shape in Pancake's way of thinking. Yes, it was a perfect square all right, and he liked it that way. Sometimes Richard enjoyed bragging about his tiny, perfect park, but there were other times when he made fun of it, especially to his cousins from the city.

A log cabin sat in the center of the park. The Boy Scouts used it for meetings, day camps, and Scout overnights. Once in awhile the Girl Scouts used it, but none of the scouts actually slept in the cabin. Instead, they camped outside in one or two-person pup tents. The Boy Scout Cabin, as everyone in town called it, was the center of the town's summertime activities, and

right next to it was a small ball diamond, Pancake's favorite place.

Summer activities at Chautauqua Park and the Boy Scout Cabin were about to begin. Richard could not wait. His mind was filled with thoughts of summer and playing ball with his friends. Of course, eating pancakes for breakfast was never far from Richard's thoughts either.

When Richard got to the park after school, the girls and Hoppy were already taking turns at batting practice. Usually the Chautauqua Park friends played by real game rules with each one getting three strikes and four balls. Richard's favorite game, Hot Box, was different. Real game rules were not as much fun as Hot Box because in Hot Box runners could keep trying until they successfully stole a base. Richard thought that batting practice and Hot Box were a blast today except that no one was very good at pitching. Batting, therefore, was not much of a challenge.

Hoppy grew tired of it.

"Hey, Pancake!" yelled Hoppy from second base where he was also trying to cover center field and play shortstop. "Go get your Dad and see if he will come pitch. He is probably better than we are, and we cannot keep this practice going much longer without a decent pitcher."

"Yeah, Pancake, go get him," echoed Skippy, who was batting at the time.

"No," said Pancake, feeling anger starting to boil inside. "I do not want him around. You want to ruin it for all of us. He is a pain in the neck."

Richard could not believe his own words. He was doing it again, making fun of Dad, just like he did when he talked about Chautauqua Park to his cousins. Why did he do that he wondered. He did not really mean it, and he knew he didn't. Yes, he was mad at Dad, that part was true. After all, he thought, Dad really is embarrassing.

The twins had to go home to supper, so Richard and Skippy and Hoppy decided to quit.

"Hey, Richard," Dad called from across the street, "Supper is ready and I've got your favorite—pancakes. Ask Hoppy to come for supper, too."

"You wanna come?" asked Richard.

"Sure," said Hoppy. "I will call Mom at work and let her know. She will not be home 'til late tonight anyway. On Mondays, she works a 12-hour shift. She is a nurse, you know, and works three 12-hour days in a row. Usually, she gets four days off, most weeks. On her 12-hour days, I am alone, but I don't mind," commented Hoppy.

Richard was thinking about all this and very much wanted Hoppy to come home with them for supper. He often wondered how Hoppy stayed so cheerful considering he did not know where his dad was. No one spoke about it much. Hoppy never did.

Pancake remembered Hoppy's remark at the bus stop that morning that at least Pancake had a dad.

"I suppose everything gets to be too much at times," Richard thought. He knew how that felt right now without Mom around. He missed their talks. He missed Mom.

"It has only been one day," said Pancake to himself. "How does Hoppy do it?"

Pancakes for Dinner

At dinner that night, Mr. Maxwell announced, "Richard. Now I want you to clean your plate. You, too, Skippy. Around here, Hoppy, that goes for everyone, so no waste. Does everyone understand?"

"Oh, no," thought Richard. "Dad is preaching again. Hoppy is going to wish he had never come to dinner."

Richard wanted to hide under the table.

It seemed to him that Dad would never quit lecturing about eating all the food on their plates. First, he made Skippy put exactly one pat of butter in the middle of each layer of pancakes; three altogether, and then pour just enough syrup to cover the cakes. Then, when they were nearly finished, he took a piece of pancake and mopped up all the leftover syrup on Richard and Skippy's plates until the plates were as clean as when the dog licks his bowl. Next, Dad ate it. Richard was dying of embarrassment inside. No one got more than half a glass of milk on a first serving either. Dad said that they might not finish it if they got a full glass.

"Why do I have to have such a weird Dad?" Richard moaned to himself.

To make matters worse, it did not look to him like Skippy or Hoppy particularly cared one way or the other about Dad's behavior.

"Why did Dad rub him the wrong way?" Richard wondered. Pancake decided that Dad was definitely odd, or O-D-D as Pancake sometimes said.

"Richard," laughed Dad, "Where are you? Are you daydreaming? We have been talking about your baseball game at the park. Yoo-hoo. Richard. Earth calling Richard. Are you there?"

Hoppy and Skippy laughed, too.

Dad continued, "Richard if you want, I will pitch for you tomorrow after school. Sounds like you kids need a pitcher."

"Sure, Dad," was all Richard could think of to say.

"I think we need more kids to play ball with us tomorrow," remarked Hoppy. "The twins help out, but we really need more to make it fun. Tomorrow at school

I will recruit some others, we will have Mr. Maxwell pitch, and it will be great!"

Skippy ran off to call the twins and find some more kids to play.

Hoppy lingered after dinner and finally decided to say what was on his mind.

"You know, Mr. Maxwell," said Hoppy, "My mom is a nurse and she says that cleaning your plate and eating more after you are full is not really very good for your body. She says it really is not a very good idea because most people just do that because someone else taught them that once. That does not make it right though. She says kids should quit eating when they are full, otherwise, they will get too fat. Then, when those fat cells are there from when we are little, it is harder to keep from getting fat when we are grownups. Mom says that if you stay slim and trim you do not get sick as often and that you will live longer. Did you ever hear of any of that, Mr. Maxwell?"

"Well, actually, yes, Hoppy. I have. Guess I never took it to heart much. You are right about the part about someone teaching us these eating habits. A lot of people my age were taught that way and even though we have learned a better way now, it is not so easy to change. As we get older, sometimes we seem to have trouble changing our habits. I like your straightforward way of telling me about it. Your mom has taught you well. I would say you are lucky to have a nurse in the family, Hoppy."

Hoppy just smiled.

Richard was not sure what just happened, but he decided it was not too bad. He did not feel quite as mad at Dad as he had. Most of the time, Richard just pretended that Dad was not there because as Richard often thought, "He never pays any attention to me anyway, so why do I care?"

Somehow, Dad's dinner conversation with Hoppy had changed things some. A little voice inside Richard's head would not leave him alone on this subject. The little voice knew that Richard really loved his Dad. "Maybe," Richard thought, "Maybe I just do not feel very loved back." Richard was not sure about that though. He would have to think about it.

As Richard lay in his bed that night, he wondered about the game tomorrow, and he wondered why things were the way they were. Richard worried, "Hoppy does not even have a Dad, and he is happy. I have a Dad, and I am miserable. When Mom is here, everything is OK. Why did she have to leave for a whole week anyway?"

The next day after school Mr. Maxwell was already at the park when Richard arrived. Mr. Maxwell was winding up on the pitcher's mound.

Richard knew he would be embarrassed if Dad threw wild pitches and hit the Boy Scout Cabin; however, Mr. Maxwell pitched rather stiffly, not wild at all. Richard commented to Hoppy, "Dad is taking this very seriously."

Valerie Vega gave Mr. Maxwell some watermelon bubble gum to chew because she said all pitchers chewed gum and that it would help him relax. Soon Mr. Maxwell started to loosen up and have some fun. Richard had to admit that he had never ever seen Dad having such a good time.

The girls recruited two more girls, and Hoppy had found four boys at school who wanted to join them. This was exactly what they needed, more players and an all-time pitcher.

When it was Richard's turn to bat, Mr.
Maxwell went through a crazy windup,
pretended to spit on the ball, and threw
Richard a fastball. No matter how mad
Pancake was at Dad, he could not help
but laugh at this serious, all-business, no-
fun, Fuddy Duddy Daddy of his who was

chewing watermelon gum, wearing his hat backwards, and doing some sort of dance on the pitcher's mound.

Mr. Maxwell and the kids were having such a good time that no one realized it was nearly 6:30, except Richard, that is, who noticed almost everything. The little brothers and sisters of some of the kids started to show up calling them home to supper. In some cases, parents came after their kids.

One of the mothers told Richard how great it was that his Dad was playing with them and that it looked like everyone was having a wonderful time. Before Richard realized what he said, he answered, "Oh, not really, it is just batting practice, and he is not much help."

"It really does not matter, Richard, just as long as you kids are having fun," the mother of one of the players said. "It sure looks like you are to me. I would not mind getting in on this myself. Are you going to be back out here tomorrow after school?" she asked.

"Yes!" yelled the kids.

"Sure," said Mr. Maxwell. "I would not miss it. Why don't you and some of the other parents join us?"

Richard went to sleep that night thinking about baseball, the park, and how silly Dad looked. He was still embarrassed by him, but maybe not quite as much.

"I think I am feeling a little better," Richard sighed as he went off to sleep. He often talked to himself at bedtime or just about any other time for that matter. "Funny thing," Pancake thought, "I don't miss Mom as bad as I did yesterday, either."

Playing Ball at the Park

By Thursday night, most of the other parents had joined their kids after school in the games at Chautauqua Park. Even Hoppy's mother was there because she had finished her shift work at the hospital for the week.

Richard's Dad, Mr. Maxwell, was having a wonderful time. He was "the life of the party" as one of the parents remarked, and the kids declared that he was their all-time pitcher.

Richard had never seen his dad like this. Most of the time, Mr. Maxwell just worked and worked and worked. Richard never remembered him playing catch or playing much of anything really. When Mr. Maxwell came home from the office, he was usually too tired to play ball, or he was off to some meeting or something, Richard recalled. He decided Dad had not changed many of his quirky habits, and Richard guessed he probably wouldn't. Somehow, all that did not matter as much anymore Richard thought to himself. Besides he was having too much fun to worry about it.

Hoppy's Mom suggested they order take-out for everyone after the game. All the parents chipped in on the cost, and the twins' Dad went to pick up the pizza. When it arrived, everyone sat around the picnic tables at the park enjoying their dinner. Richard could not remember feeling so good for a long, long time.

That night when Pancake was about ready for bed, Mr. Maxwell came up to his room to talk some more about the games at the park.

"You know, Richard," Mr. Maxwell said, "I feel like I have been on vacation all week. I have not had this much fun in years. I feel like a kid again thanks to you and your friends. Tomorrow, your Mom comes back, and I will be glad for sure. Still, I am happy to have had such a great week with you kids. I know it is not easy putting up with my boring ways and me. I feel 10 years younger. I had forgotten how to play and how to enjoy myself. You kids helped me remember how to do that. Well, good night Bud. See you in the morning."

Mr. Maxwell left the room quietly; he had never been one for hugs and stuff at bedtime. Maybe that would change, too, Richard thought, or maybe not. It did not seem as important any more.

"Wait a minute," Richard said out loud to himself, "Did Dad just call me 'Bud'? A new nickname maybe?"

Richard lay awake a long time that night since he had a lot to think about, especially Dad.

Richard thought, "Dad is still the same old Dad all right. He is still odd about some things he does--pretty weird, actually. This has been a great week though, and Mom comes home tomorrow. I think I like Dad a lot better. Things are definitely not going to be quite the same around here anymore." Richard decided all this as he watched his favorite sports shows on television, listened to spring preseason baseball scores, and as usual, dreamed about stealing second base.

A New Nickname for Dad

Mom arrived home about 9 on Friday night just after the weary Chautauqua Park baseball players had finished a quick supper of scrambled eggs, turkey bacon, toast, and pancakes made with skim milk and served with only one pat of butter. Mr. Maxwell was now on a health-eating crusade after Hoppy had convinced him of the perils of eating too much fat and sugar. As Mr. Maxwell talked about healthy foods, Richard thought to himself, "Well, he is still lecturing, but this time it is not so bad, I guess."

Pancake had leg cramps after the extra exercise all week, and he was bone tired. He did not mind, though, because he could hit Dad's pitches now. Pancake hurried his bath and climbed into bed. His legs ached worse than ever. About then, Mom tiptoed into his room to tell him hello and goodnight all at the same time. Richard was glad to see her but too tired to talk much. He briefly told his mom about the week and Dad and baseball. Pancake sleepily said something to his mother about his dad not being such a Fuddy Duddy Daddy anymore and that Dad actually called Hoppy by his nickname now instead of Thomas Arlen Vincent II.

"Really Richard," Mom said with surprise as she told Richard goodnight. "I am so glad for all of you, but I am especially happy for Dad. I bet you kids did not know that he used to be quite the baseball player. Kids called him 'Cotton' then."

Richard was almost asleep, but he had to ask, "Why did they call him 'Cotton', Mom? You never told us."

"Well, it was because he was pitching and blowing a bubble when some little pieces of cotton-like seeds from a

cottonwood tree were flying through the air. Some of them got stuck on his bubble, which was huge, and then the bubble popped. Dad got cottonwood seeds and bubble gum all over his face and hat and never lived it down. Everyone called him 'Cotton' after that," Mrs. Maxwell said.

Pancake smiled as he fell asleep that night. His Fuddy Daddy Daddy had a nickname, too. Tomorrow, Pancake decided he would call him Cotton to see what he would do. "Funny thing about nicknames," Richard thought, "somehow nicknames make people a lot more fun to know."

Richard yawned and just before he fell asleep he decided that he would definitely have pancakes for breakfast in the morning.

Richard Austin Maxwell was always thinking.

THE END